Dolphins in Danger

Adventures of Riley™

Dolphins in Danger

Dear Riley,
My friend Dr. Poole, an expert on dolphins and whales, has invited us to the South Pacific island of Moorea to study spinner dolphin behavior and communication.
Do you know how spinners get their name? Dr. Poole will explain that and a whole lot more! Aunt Martha, Cousin Alice, and I can't wait to go. See you soon in a dolphin **lagoon**!

Uncle Max

BY **Amanda Lumry**

AND **Laura Hurwitz**

ILLUSTRATED BY **Sarah McIntyre**

SCHOLASTIC PRESS ★ NEW YORK

A special thank-you to all the scientists who collaborated on this project. Your time and assistance are very much appreciated.

First published in China in 2005 by Eaglemont Press.
www.eaglemont.com

All photographs by Amanda Lumry except:
Pages 10–11 humpback whale © Rod Haestier/Getty Images
Pages 14–15 spinner dolphin © Tim Davis/Getty Images
Page 29 spinner dolphin © Dr. Michael Poole

Illustrations © 2005 by Sarah McIntyre
Editing and Digital Compositing by Michael E. Penman
Digital Imaging by Embassy Graphics, Canada

Library of Congress Control Number: 2004019519

ISBN-13: 978-0-545-06839-0
ISBN-10: 0-545-06839-8

10 9 8 7 6 5 4 3 2 1   09 10 11 12 13

Printed in Singapore   46
First Scholastic printing, February 2009

FSC
Mixed Sources
Product group from well-managed forests, controlled sources and recycled wood or fibre
Cert no. DNV-COC-000025
www.fsc.org
© 1996 Forest Stewardship Council

A portion of the proceeds from your purchase of this licensed product supports the stated educational mission of the Smithsonian Institution— "the increase and diffusion of knowledge." The name of the Smithsonian Institution and the sunburst logo are registered trademarks of the Smithsonian Institution and are registered in the U.S. Patent and Trademark Office. www.si.edu

2% of the proceeds from this book will be donated to the Wildlife Conservation Society. http://wcs.org

An average royalty of approximately 3 cents from the sale of each book in the Adventures of Riley series will be received by World Wildlife Fund (WWF) to support their international efforts to protect endangered species and their habitats. ® WWF Registered Trademark Panda Symbol © 1986 WWF. © 1986 Panda symbol WWF-World Wide Fund For Nature (also known as World Wildlife Fund) ® "WWF" is a WWF Registered Trademark © 1986 WWF-Fonds Mondial pour la Nature symbole du panda Marque Déposée du WWF ®
www.worldwildlife.org

We try to produce the most beautiful books possible and we are extremely concerned about the impact of our manufacturing process on the forests of the world and the environment as a whole. Accordingly, we made sure that the paper used in this book has been certified as coming from forests that are managed to ensure the protection of the people and wildlife dependent upon them.

Tweeeet!
Tweet!

"For my trip, I need to practice surfing and talking to dolphins," said Riley.

"They won't understand you," said Riley's friend Mike.

"Sure they will," said Riley. "People use whistles to teach dolphins tricks, don't they? I'm going to use my whistle to train the dolphins in Moorea (Moh-oh-ray-ah)."

When they landed in Moorea, it was midday and very hot.

"*Ia Orana* (Ya-or-ah-nah)! That's Tahitian for hello," Dr. Michael Poole greeted them.

"When can we see the dolphins?" asked Alice.

"If we hurry, we can spot them swimming in the **lagoon** right now," said Dr. Poole.

"Then I can teach them to do some tricks," Riley whispered to Alice.

Arrivée

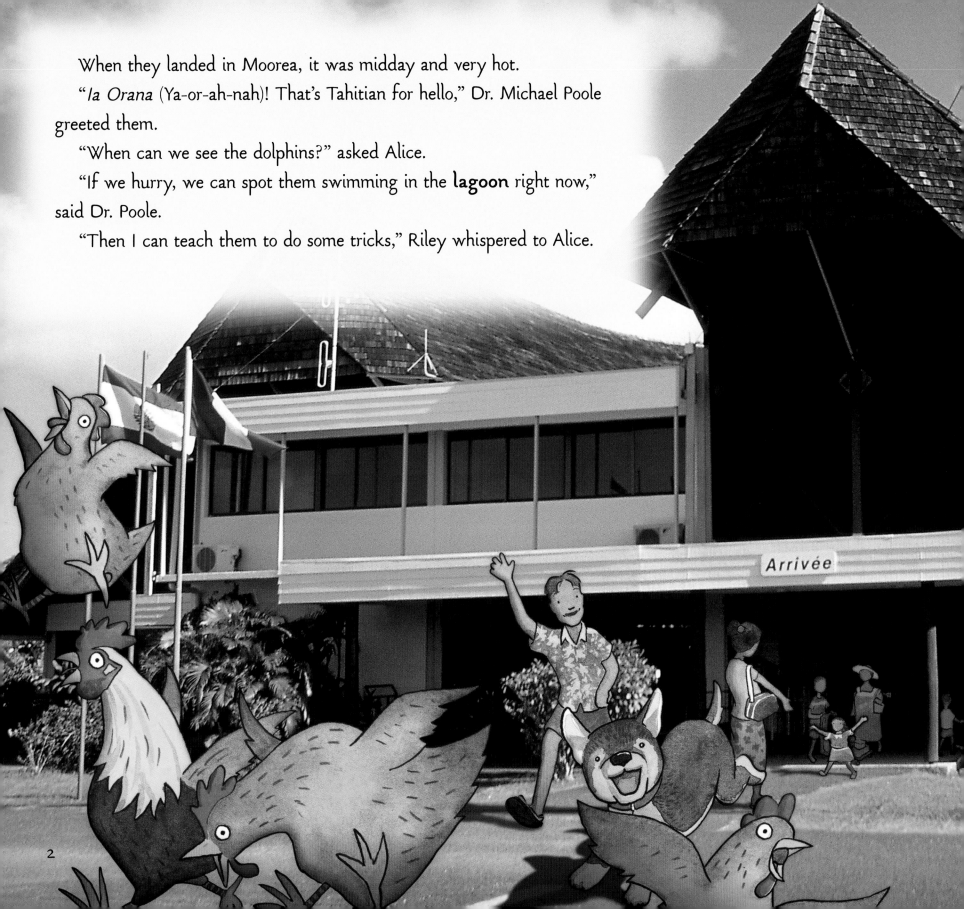

2

> It is about as large as all of Earth's other oceans combined.
> It is the largest and deepest ocean.
> Pacific means "peaceful."

—Dr. Paul Boyle, Director, New York Aquarium, Wildlife Conservation Society

Pacific Ocean

3

"I can't wait to see the show!" said Alice as everyone climbed into the boat.
"What show?" asked Aunt Martha.

4

"The dolphin show," said Riley. "You know, where they do tricks."

"This isn't a theme park," said Uncle Max. "These are wild dolphins in their natural **environment**."

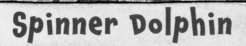

Spinner Dolphin

➤ A dolphin travels in small schools (2–40 dolphins) called pods, or larger schools of up to several hundred members, called herds.

➤ A dolphin is a mammal, not a fish, and must breathe air to survive.

➤ It can swim up to 25 mph (40 km/h)!

—Lisette Wilson, South Pacific Regional Marine Coordinator, World Wildlife Fund

SPLASH!

A dolphin leaped high in front of them.

"Wow!" said Riley. Another dolphin twirled in the air. Riley and Alice clapped.

"How did you teach them to do that, Dr. Poole?" asked Alice.

"I bet you used a whistle!" added Riley.

Laughing, Dr. Poole said, "Spinning is how spinner dolphins get their name! They spin to remove remoras, which are fish that attach themselves to the dolphin's skin. They also jump as part of a playtime, like school recess. It is my job to study and learn from the dolphins, not to teach them anything. Hmm . . . I don't know how the dolphins got in here. The nearest **lagoon** opening from the ocean is very shallow and narrow, and I've never seen them use it before."

Lagoon Diagram

New Islands

Main Island

Lagoon

Coral Reef

Openings

Coral Reef

Ocean

"That dolphin is missing part of its **dorsal** fin," noticed Uncle Max.

"That's Shark Bite," said Dr. Poole. "It was in a fight with a shark. To keep track of the dolphins, I give them names that I won't forget."

At dinner, they met Dr. Poole's sons, Temoana (Tay-mo-ah-nah) and Tearenui (Tay-ah-ray-noo-ee), and his wife, Mareva (Mah-ray-vah). The boys promised to take Riley and Alice surfing the next morning.

Breadfruit

➤ Breadfruit is usually oblong and large, weighing 10 pounds (4.5 kg) or more when ripe.

➤ Breadfruit is a member of the fig family.

➤ When roasted, breadfruit looks like freshly baked bread.

—Dr. Warren Wagner, Botany Curator, Smithsonian Institution

8

"Surf's up!" yelled Alice, as she zoomed by Riley.

"It sure looks easier on TV," said Riley, as he wiped out again.

"Alice! You're a natural!" said Temoana.

I wish I was a better surfer, thought Riley.

"Look!" said Tearenui. "Humpback whales! They always return this time of year to have their babies. Let's go tell Papa."

"That whale is bigger than our boat," said Alice. "I hope it doesn't tip us over!"

"Accidents can happen if people approach whales too quickly or get too close, but if we respect them and give them some space, there is really very little danger," said Dr. Poole.

"I read that humpbacks can sing," said Riley.

"True," said Aunt Martha.

"The songs they use to **communicate** are beautiful."

"When they sing, they point their heads straight down toward the ocean floor," added Dr. Poole.

"Cool!" said Riley and Alice.

"Hey, did you know that I can speak dolphin?" said Riley. He blew his whistle—*loudly.*

"OW! My ears!" said Alice.

Humpback Whale

➤ A whale's flippers are one-third the length of its body.

➤ It **migrates** 2,000–3,000 miles (3,200–4,800 km) per year between colder waters and warmer waters.

➤ A baby humpback, called a calf, can weigh up to 3,000 pounds (1,360 kg).

—Dr. Howard Rosenbaum, Director, Cetacean Conservation Program, Wildlife Conservation Society

"I think the dolphins would agree with you, Alice!" said Dr. Poole. "A plastic whistle just makes a loud noise that doesn't mean anything to them. Dolphins use special sounds when inter-acting with each other and to measure the size and location of an object. They may also **communicate** by the way they twirl and spin."

After watching the giant whales **breach** and blow,
everyone cooled off in the **lagoon**
and explored the world below.

Manta Ray

➤ It can weigh over 6,600 pounds (3,000 kg) and have a wingspan over 26 ft. (8 m)!

➤ A manta ray can jump completely out of the water.

➤ It eats plankton, small shrimp, or fish.

—Paul Sieswerda, Aquarium Curator, New York Aquarium, Wildlife Conservation Society

Parrot Fish

➤ Its top and bottom front teeth grow together to form a beak.

➤ It uses its beak to bite off pieces of coral and eat the plants growing on them.

—Dr. Victor G. Springer, Senior Scientist, Division of Fishes, Smithsonian Institution

➤ There are over 200 species of moray eels, and scientists are still discovering new ones.

➤ An eel can grow over 6 ft. (1.8 m) long and may weigh over 100 pounds (45 kg).

➤ It doesn't usually bite humans, unless it is surprised or bothered.

—Dr. David G. Smith, Museum Specialist, National Museum of Natural History, Smithsonian Institution

Moray Eel

> A grouper is usually born as a female, but may turn into a male after a year or more.

> Lunging out from its coral hiding place, with a snap of its jaws it catches its prey in less than a second.

—Dr. Carole Baldwin, Research Zoologist, Smithsonian Institution

Grouper

"Spinner dolphins!" cried Aunt Martha.

"That's odd," said Dr. Poole. "They should have gone out to the ocean to feed last night, and then returned to another part of the **lagoon** today. Something is wrong. We'd better get back to the lab. I should check my photos to see if these are the same dolphins we saw yesterday. They may be trapped in the lagoon and could starve. The food they need to survive can only be found out in the open ocean."

14

As Uncle Max and Dr. Poole hurried off, the others stayed behind with Mareva. "I practice Tahitian dances every Friday night," she told them. "Would you like to join me?"

"Sure!" Alice nodded excitedly. "I love to dance!"

Vanilla

➤ The vanilla plant is actually an orchid. Vanilla comes from a long, beanlike fruit produced on its vines.

➤ The small black spots you see in some kinds of vanilla ice cream are the tiny seeds from inside the orchid bean.

—John Kress, Research Scientist and Curator, Department of Botany, Smithsonian Institution

I can't dance or surf like Alice. Is there anything I'm good at? thought Riley. "I think I'll go and see what Uncle Max and Dr. Poole are doing."

17

On his way to the lab, Riley saw Temoana's surfboard. *If I practice, I know I can be as good as Alice.* Riley walked along the beach until he saw some small waves out past the **lagoon**.

Passes (Openings)

Moorea

Ocean

Lagoon

He steered through
the opening into the
breaking waves.

19

Riley crashed headfirst into the water. Gasping, he **panicked**! Which way was up? Was it his imagination, or did he see a dark shape coming toward him?

A gentle **nudge** pushed him to the surface. *Brrrp! Blah!* Salt water **gushed** out of his mouth. Suddenly, he felt himself being pulled from the water.

"Thank heavens we noticed the surfboard was missing and found you!" cried Aunt Martha.

"The surf out here by the **coral reef** is very dangerous!" said Dr. Poole.

"I know that *now*," said a red-faced Riley, rubbing his head. "But how did I get back to the surfboard?"

"Let me guess, you were saved by the dolphins," said Alice, laughing.

"No, really," said Riley. "I think I was."

"These are the same dolphins from yesterday. They look very tired and hungry," Dr. Poole said.

"I could blow my whistle!" said Riley. "If we make enough noise, they might be happy to leave."

"Good idea," said Dr. Poole. "But we may need some help in case they swim the wrong way."

24

"What about a *hukilau*?" asked Aunt Martha.

"A what?" asked Alice.

"A *hukilau* works like a net, but is just a rope with palm leaves hanging from it, so there is no danger of a dolphin's fins getting caught," said Aunt Martha. "I saw one in Hawaii."

Dr. Poole called for help.

Soon the **lagoon** was full of boats! They formed two lines. The first line was full of dancers with metal pipes and paddles to bang underwater. Behind them were fishermen with a long *hukilau* net.

"Riley, now's your chance! Blow your whistle to start our dolphin parade!" said Dr. Poole.

Tweeet!
Tweet!
Clang!
Bang!
Splash!
Splash!
Clang!
Bang!

At first nothing happened. Then, slowly, one dolphin swam forward, then another, and another. Soon the dolphins were at the opening. In a flash, they were gone, leaving the **lagoon** behind.

Spinner Dolphin

➤ A dolphin can dive 1,000 ft. (300 m) deep—that's like diving off a 100-story building!

➤ 6–8 million dolphins, including spinners, have been caught and killed in the EASTERN Pacific Ocean since 1970 as a result of **purse seine net fishing**.

➤ It can spin up to 7 times in a single jump!

—Dr. Michael Poole, Director, Marine Mammal Research Program, CRIOBE

"Look!" cried Riley.

Shark Bite leaped up right in front of him, spinning in the air. Everyone cheered. The dolphins were saved!

29

That night, they watched Mareva dance.
"You're a great dancer," said Riley. "Unlike me."
"Thank you," Mareva said. "And you are an excellent scientist. You knew just how to save those dolphins. We all have talents, but sometimes we don't know it until the right moment comes along." Riley blushed.

Black Pearl

➤ A pearl is usually the same color as the mollusk that produced it.

➤ Pearls come in all shapes and sizes. Round ones are rare.

➤ An adult pearl oyster can pump over 5 gal. (19 L) of water through its gills every hour.

—Mona Matepi,
Project Officer,
World Wildlife
Fund, Cook Islands

"Nets and loud noises can be used to trap and kill dolphins," said Dr. Poole. "Today we used these things to save their lives. By studying how dolphins behave and **communicate**, we hope to find even more ways to help them."

"And maybe they'll teach us a thing or two along the way," said Riley.

Back home, Riley entertained everyone with his amazing dolphin rescue story. At the beach, he showed his family his new surfing skills. His father took pictures, which Riley sent to Alice. He returned to living the life of a nine-year-old, until he once again heard from Uncle Max.

Where will Riley go next?

FURTHER INFORMATION

French Polynesia

Bora Bora

Huahine

Tahaa

Raiatea

Moorea

Papeete

Tahiti

Pacific Ocean

N
W   E
S

Dr. Michael Poole is a real scientist! An American marine biologist, he came to Moorea in 1987. In real life he is married to Mareva, who really is a Tahitian dancer, and they do have two sons, Temoana and Tearenui.

Dr. Poole is known around the world for his work with spinner dolphins and humpback whales. He helped create one of the largest dolphin and whale sanctuaries in the world, to protect the marine mammals in French Polynesian waters.

Glossary

breach: to leap out of the water and land back with a splash

communicate: to give information or messages by talking or moving

coral reef: a grouping of coral that forms a home for fish

dorsal: on or near the back

environment: the space where an animal lives, sleeps, and eats

gushed: poured or flowed quickly and all at once

lagoon: an area of water separated from the sea or ocean, often by a coral reef or piece of land

migrates: travels from one place to another, usually during a change of seasons

nudge: to push gently

panicked: showing sudden fear

purse seine net fishing: a method used to catch tuna, using a net that is a mile long and several hundred feet deep. The net closes like a drawstring purse around the tuna and anything else in the area. The fishermen are supposed to give dolphins a chance to escape, but a mistake in a single fishing haul can mean the death or injury of 500 to 2,000 dolphins

starve: to become weak due to lack of food

Coral

Careful! Coral is alive and part of the reef. Touching or stepping on it can damage or even kill it. Without coral, fish have no reason to stay, and we would have nothing left to see.

Surfing Lesson: Riding waves while lying on a wooden board started in the Polynesian Islands over 3,000 years ago. The first surfers were fisherman using *paipo* (known today as body boards) to ride waves back to shore, along with any fish they caught. Over time, riding waves became a pastime and not just a part of the fisherman's job.

JOIN US FOR MORE GREAT ADVENTURES!